IN THE BLINK
OF AN EYE

BY

RUFARO

This factual fiction narrative provides an insightful look into the life experiences of different characters as they navigate their way through a global pandemic. The pandemic has, without a doubt created massive disruptions to all spheres of life.

ACKNOWLEDGEMENTS

To my immediate family, I'm grateful for your love, prayers and encouragement throughout these challenging times.

Living through a global pandemic has been life-altering, BUT I remain incredibly grateful to GOD for his unconditional LOVE and GRACE. As the saying goes "God never leads us into a storm he doesn't give us the power to OVERCOME"

TABLE OF CONTENTS

CHAPTER ONE:

———∞———

A JOYFUL REUNION!

It's 6.30 am, and my alarm has already been going off at least three times! I have to leave the house by precisely 8 am. Will I make it? Only God knows. Being punctual has never been my strongest point; I'm always late for one reason or another. However, on this occasion; I couldn't afford to be late. I had been invited to spend a few weeks with my cousin, Tatenda and his wonderful mum, Aunty Joy in London. The trip was a great escape away from my hectic and sometimes stressful life in Harare. Two years ago, I graduated from the University of Zimbabwe with a 1st class degree in Economics. Still, since jobs are scarce, I decided to use a small loan I received from my best friend, Joseph to open a clothing boutique. So far, the boutique has proven to be a great success as it's frequently visited by the who's who of Harare; but it's no surprise as I am the most fashionable young lady in town! The extra income has enabled me to hire an assistant; a young eccentric lady named Juliet, to help with running the shop. She's a natural salesperson and the customers love her witty sense of humour. Upon learning about my visit to London, Juliet couldn't contain her excitement. "Aunty, do you mean you will be living right next to white people, walking on the same road too?" she asked burning with curiosity. I looked at her bemused, wondering how I had ended up with such a comical assistant.

A few days later I had finished packing up all my suitcases ready to depart.

"Nashe, if you do not get in the car within the next 20 minutes, you will be walking to London," my mother yelled at me as she reached for her shoes. She, without a doubt, was one of the most punctual people I had ever known. However, she had somehow raised the most non-punctual daughter ever, me! At precisely 7.45 am (fifteen minutes ahead of schedule), I was sitting in the car buckled up and raring to go. Although the airport was quite a distance away from our house, we still had enough time to get there. My feelings were a mixture of fear, anxiety and excitement. I had always been a nervous flyer and the thought of cruising 33,000 feet above sea level filled me with deep anxiety. The fact that my younger sister kept on talking about plane crashes didn't help either, "Nashe, are you sure about flying with that airline, especially after their recent air crash?" Farai asked with great curiosity. I'm not easily annoyed, but she always knew how to get under my skin, with her unnecessary questions. "Don't speak such negativity over your sister's life; words have power," Mum scolded Farai as she reached to grab her case of gospel CDs.

She started singing along and instructed me to command the spirit of fear to leave me. "Mum, don't you think you're going overboard with all this? I'm fine, just a little anxious that's all," I voiced. Completely disregarding my comment, she continued to sing and pray along until ten minutes later when the car came to a halt at the traffic lights. Finally, she opened her mouth to speak,

"There is no such thing as going overboard when it comes to worshipping God." Once she got into the *worshipping mood* there was no way to stop her. She would continue to sing until she lost her voice! As soon as we arrived at the airport, I said my final goodbyes and headed straight to the departures area. When I finally boarded the plane, I couldn't contain my excitement. Although I was going to miss my family and crazy customers, the thought of spending quality time with Aunty Joy and Tatenda filled me with great happiness.

14hours and two flights later, I finally arrived in London, the city that never sleeps. To say I was tired was simply an understatement; my body ached, and the freezing weather didn't help either. The check-out process was much quicker than I anticipated and before you know it, I was sitting on the sofa in my Aunt's living room, drinking a tasty hot chocolate. Aunty Joy, whom I could tell was eager to feed me with all the food she could find, was already in the kitchen cooking up a feast. I was sitting comfortably, smiling in delighted anticipation of the treat ahead. Although we lived thousands of miles apart, we had always kept in contact, never missing a birthday, anniversary, and other important life milestones. I received nothing short of a joyous welcome. We talked, laughed and reminisced about the good old days for hours until Tatenda had to leave for his night shift. For as long as I had known Tatenda, he had always been very career-driven, focused on nothing else but his profession as a medical doctor. The idea of getting married and having kids never really appealed to him. His nonchalant attitude towards marriage annoyed his mother, who never failed to remind him at any given opportunity that he was no longer 'a spring chicken' but an 'aged hen' that needed to give her grandchildren. "All your cousin ever thinks about is work, work and travelling across the globe, forgetting that time is running out. He's getting older and I want to see my grandkids before God takes me back," she murmured. Although this exchange amused me, I was never one to get involved in disputes between family members, so in true Nashe style, I stirred the conversation back to food. "Aunty, your cooking gets better and better every time; you must teach me some of the recipes before I go back home," I said joyfully. The frown on her face slowly turned into a smile; after all, she loved to receive compliments. "Back in my days, Nashe, I was the supreme Queen of everything, I sang, danced and my cooking skills were always the talk of the town," Aunty reminisced. She was indeed her own biggest cheerleader!

The following day I woke up around mid-day after a much-needed rest. Aunty Joy had already set out the plans of what we would be doing. She had taken a whole week off from work, so we could spend some quality time together, gallivanting around the beautiful city of London. Although it was my third time visiting, I always felt in awe of its stunning architecture, bright lights, and fast-moving trains! The weather took me a bit longer to adjust to, considering that I was coming from the blazing hot city of Harare. Tatenda had surprised me with a brand new camera, which came in handy during our city escapades. With his hectic schedule, we rarely ever got the chance to spend quality time together. However, he finally managed to take a couple of days off and show me the nightlife in London. Going out and exploring London in the evening was an experience to remember. We dined at some lavish restaurants, which I thoroughly enjoyed considering that food is my second specialty after fashion, of course!

One morning, I found a handwritten note on the dinner table Aunty Joy had left for me. The message read, "Good morning darling, I have gone to work and will be coming back at 6 pm; there's rice and stew in the fridge. Your cousin *Mr. save the world* will be returning from his night shift around 11am." I loved being in Aunty Joy's company, but she was at times very talkative, so to be able to sit in solitude for a few hours was a welcome relief. Just as I was starting to enjoy my alone time, listening to the chirping birds outside, Tatenda walked in. He looked deflated as if he had been run over by a train, definitely not the same classy and jovial guy that I had seen the previous evening. My mind started racing, wondering what could have happened. Did he wrongfully diagnose one of his patients? Or maybe something terrible had happened to Aunty Joy. "Is everything okay, bro? You seem troubled" I asked in a very concerned tone. "I'm fine, just a bit shook by the news I read online on my way here," Tatenda expressed as he took a deep breath.

CHAPTER TWO:

IN THE BLINK OF AN EYE

"A new virus, Covid-19, which they are saying, greatly affects the respiratory system has been discovered here in the UK," Tatenda revealed. "Sounds to me like a lab experiment gone wrong; the name itself says it all," I joked.

I had a quick glance at Tatenda, who was engrossed in reading article after article, trying to figure out more about this supposedly unique virus. He clearly didn't see the humour in the joke I had made earlier. "If this isn't contained as quickly as possible many lives will be lost; I can just imagine the pressure we are going to be under at the hospital," he expressed. When he mentioned about people losing their lives and livelihoods, I realized that this was no laughing matter. Life as we knew it was about to change drastically.

An hour later, Aunty Joy returned from work, completely oblivious to the situation at hand "the silence in this house is deafening; what's with the long faces? Tatenda, your face is long enough; don't make it any longer", she said with witticism. For a second, my mind drifted away and I burst into laughter, completely disregarding the concerning situation at hand. Tatenda explained to her about this newly found virus but being the strong woman of faith that she's, her response was simply, "so all of you are sitting here trembling in fear, where is your faith in God?" She was right, but this was clearly not the time to start such a conversation.

After the media officially announced that we were now living in a global pandemic, some dismissed this information as untrue and attempted to continue living normally as if nothing had changed. Governments began recommending wearing face masks, temperature screening and social distancing to prevent the virus from spreading. Freedom of movement immediately became a thing of the past. Airplanes were grounded, which meant that my stay in London was extended. I kept in contact with my mum and sister as I watched the world change. As governments continued to impose strict restrictions on movement, people's livelihoods and routines were disrupted, leading to higher levels of stress, loneliness and other challenges. For many, the unpredictability of the virus heightened their anxiety levels and depression.

Across the world, public spaces such as schools, local shops and places of worship were ordered to close down with immediate effect. Since churches were closed, we had to resort to watching online services. This somehow helped, though it didn't feel the same as being physically present in the church. However, I felt better knowing that I didn't have to be physically present to be able to talk to God. As long as I had faith, he would hear me wherever I was. Each day I dreaded what would happen next but kept holding onto the belief that none of my family members would succumb to the virus. I would later discover how wrong I was.

As the pandemic progressed, hospitals in most parts of Europe were overwhelmed with Covid-19 patients; it appeared that no one really knew how to combat it. All that the governments and scientists could do was advice the public to take precautions such as wearing masks, staying indoors and social distancing. Unfortunately, as a medical doctor, Tatenda was part of the frontline staff dealing with severely ill Covid-19 patients. They were times he wouldn't return home for days, which left us deeply worried.

Unbeknown to us, Tatenda had also been struggling with his mental health for a long time. To be frank, there's a small part of me that had always been envious of Tatenda. He seemed to have it ALL together on the outside but little did I know that internally, his mental well-being was deteriorating. He had invested so much in his outer appearance as a way of hiding the internal battles he struggled with daily. Being a man and knowing how men have always been taught to be strong, I understood why he desperately wanted to paint a happy picture. I came from an environment where mental health-related issues were rarely discussed. If you are a man, you had to toughen up and for women; we were always encouraged to fight our battles through prayer.

One fateful evening, Tatenda finally broke down in my presence. He had been working tirelessly at the hospital, and it was all starting to take a massive toll on him. He began to cry profusely, "Nashe, I don't think I can continue living this life anymore," I could feel the tears building up inside me and tried my best to stop them from falling down. This was a breakthrough moment, one which rarely ever occurred. I was ready to lend an ear and assured him that whatever it was, my perception of him as a great young man was never going to change.

"At work, I walk around from ward to ward, watching people take their last breath and wondering whether I will be the next to go. I'm supposed to give patients hope, to be the light in their moment of darkness, but how can I be the light when my heart is heavy with darkness? Each day I come across frail patients held hostage by Covid-19 and reassure them that all will be well. I fight back the tears because once again, I'm reminded that I'm a MAN and men don't cry or show emotions in public.

My mother showers me with compliments; "you're such a brave young man, just like your father."

I look at her and fake a smile. Deep inside me, I don't want her to tell me how brave I am or that I'm just like my father; instead, I long to hear her say, "son, if you ever feel like crying, letting it all out, know that it's okay, there's no shame in that."

At night, I lay awake engulfed by inexplicable fear and anxiety, twisting and turning, wishing I could escape from my own skin. Counting each breath I take, thinking if I close my eyes, will I ever open them again.

But I tell myself, you're a man, be strong, men aren't supposed to cry or crumble in fear.

When the sun rises, I somehow find the strength to get up and get ready to face the day. I look in the mirror, and all I can hear is society telling me to be fearless, but all I want is for someone to hold my hand, breathe life into me and say it's going to be okay." **Tatenda**

As I sat there, holding his hand tightly, I realized that men suffer internally too, just like us women. It became evident to me why my mother had always emphasized the need to be KIND as you never know the internal battles someone could be facing. In rare instances where a person decided to speak out about their internal struggles in my community, prayer was usually the first suggested solution. So I proceeded to set out a prayer plan, which I believed would help him overcome the demons stealing away his joy and peace of mind. We would dedicate many hours to prayer sessions, but I could feel him sinking back into the depression a few days after. While prayer works, I realized that there are also other tools like therapy, which together with prayer, bring positive outcomes. As the saying goes, "prayer is a weapon AND therapy is a strategy." Not only therapy but simple things like exercising, healthy eating and spending quality time doing things you enjoy with loved ones along with PRAYING definitely makes a huge difference.

Let me take this moment to ask you a few questions:

- Do you feel like your mental well-being has in any way been affected as a result of living through a global pandemic?

- What would you say has been the greatest challenge or life lesson you have learned during the pandemic?

CHAPTER THREE:

---∽∞∽---

ALL THAT GLITTERS IS NOT GOLD (PART 1)

Aunty Joy had managed to buy a beautiful house in one of London's most expensive neighborhoods. As amazing as it was, I found it to be very quiet; you could easily go for weeks without seeing your neighbours. I truly missed the fun interactions I had with my neighbours back home in Harare. Everyone was always in each other's business; you knew who was dating who, how the Aunty who lived down the street had been caught with another man while her husband was away, all sorts of interesting stories. Regardless of the hardships we faced, there was never a dull moment, always something to gossip about or laugh at. Your neighbours were practically like a second family and for some people, the only family they had ever known. However, in this London neighborhood everyone seemed to be solely focused on their own lives.

"Beautiful, fashionable, hair down to her back like Rapunzel," this was Sarah, Aunty Joy's neighbor. Likewise, her husband was handsome, tall; every time he smiled, it was as if the gates of heaven had opened up. I had never seen a man with such shiny and white teeth before. "Tatenda, I don't think the man next door is real because those teeth it's like the angels in heaven come down and brush them for him," I said jokingly. Both Tatenda and Aunty Joy laughed hysterically. Adding to his amazing physical appearance, he had amassed a lot of wealth through his property investment company. They had been blessed with two beautiful young children and his wife Sarah was the perfect pampered housewife. From the outside, they looked like the perfect couple and family. Although she was a full-time housewife, Sarah was always strolling around the house in her trendy fashions. "What prayers do I have to say to get such a perfect lifestyle because I'm tired of working hard 24/7 and still living an ordinary life?" I asked curiously. Being the King of wisdom, Tatenda simply said, "Nashe, all that glitters is not gold, you don't know what goes on behind closed doors, so don't be quick to envy people's lives based on outward appearances."

However, being naturally inquisitive, my mind began to wonder. When life was still "normal" before the never-ending cycle of lockdowns came into force, we rarely ever saw Sarah outside of the house. Did she just enjoy being inside the house, or was it down to something more sinister? I wondered. I usually had strong instincts about people, but there had been occasions in the past when my instincts had misled me.

Surely, a housewife that's at home 24/7 would welcome the opportunity to step outside, meet up with a friend or just run errands instead of staying all day locked up inside. She would only leave the house to welcome her husband home every evening.

On the rare occasion I would see her, she always had this worried look and would try her best to keep the conversation at a minimum, rushing to go back inside the house. "Don't mind her as long as we have lived in this neighborhood; she has always been very dismissive and ignorant. I'm telling you her demons are huge; she needs spiritual deliverance," revealed Aunty Joy. As the saying goes, "You can take the woman out of Africa, but you cannot take the African out of the woman." Although she had lived in England for decades, she still held onto the mentality some of our elders had; the devil and his demons were always to blame. Lack of manors or respect is perceived as either a sign of poor home training or that you are somehow possessed with serious demons prohibiting you from living in harmony with others. "What can she be depressed about? After all, she's married to a wealthy and seemingly generous husband," I thought quietly to myself. Maybe Aunty Joy was right after all; being possessed by demons seemed to be the only logical answer.

Weeks went by, and I had reluctantly settled into my new reality. I spent most of my days indoors watching movies, reading the bible, checking up on my family back in Harare and going for short walks around the neighbourhood with Aunty Joy to get some fresh air. Every time Aunty Joy and I would walk past Sarah's house, I was secretly hoping that we would see her; so we could try and have a lengthy conversation. My mind was filled with many questions, which only Sarah could provide the answers to. We barely knew each other and like my mother always warned me, "stay out of people's business," so I tried to stop obsessing with finding out what was or wasn't happening in her life.

However, her husband, Dave seemed to be more friendly and approachable. During the weekends, when he was taking his kids to their tennis lessons before the pandemic started, he would always engage in a lengthy conversation with Aunty Joy. I would hear them exchanging pleasantries. She finally introduced me to him one Saturday afternoon and he appeared to be very friendly. "He's such a great and very hard-working man, such a shame he married that rude and lazy woman who does nothing but stay indoors spending all his money on clothes," she said with a sigh of irritation. "Mum, you need to refrain from making negative remarks towards Sarah; we don't even know what goes on behind closed doors; maybe she's going through a hard time," Tatenda refuted. He was right; maybe we had been overly judgmental towards Sarah without thinking deeply about other potential reasons behind her anti-social and dismissive attitude. As the saying goes, "there's more to a person than what meets the eye," and little did we know that the truth was to reveal itself much sooner.

Like many others, when the country was placed under a national lockdown, Dave worked from home instead of going to his office; the same applied to Aunty Joy. Every day after midnight, we would always hear strange sounds coming from Dave and Sarah's house; it sounded like something was being hit against the wall. "Dave did say that they have a small gym set up in their basement; maybe it's probably just him working out and throwing around his equipment," Aunty Joy disclosed. It sounded like a valid reason; considering his perfect physique, it was clear that Dave spent a lot of time exercising. He worked long hours, which I believed left him with very little time to exercise during the day. However, as the days went by, the sounds became louder and louder, "Aunty, maybe next time you speak to Dave, you should mention this to him because I'm starting to get concerned," I voiced. Once again, my mind began to wonder, maybe they're holding people hostage in their basement or running some illegal factory. I had seen such things happen so many times in movies and to think something similar was possibly happening right next door made me anxious. As for Aunty Joy, she already planned to call her pastor, asking for some anointing oil and prayers. Anointing oil combined with a heartfelt prayer were her solutions to every problem she encountered. "For all we know, they could be practicing witchcraft, so it's best we cover ourselves with the blood of Jesus to prohibit any evil spirits from entering our home," she expressed.

Tatenda and I both laughed hysterically, but going by her serious facial expression; she was clearly unimpressed.

CHAPTER FOUR:

ALL THAT GLITTERS IS NOT GOLD (PART 2)

D ays went by and Sarah or her children were nowhere to be seen. We would only see Dave early in the morning taking the bins out. Since the schools were closed, their children had always spent lunchtime playing in the backyard, but this was no longer the case. Although Sarah hardly ever left the house, she did use to step outside at least for some minutes, but it's like she had strangely disappeared into thin air.

Oddly enough, the loud sounds which always intensified during midnight still continued. However, they seemed to be more violent during one evening, as if a real struggle was taking place between two people. Filled with deep worry and curiosity my mind wouldn't allow me to rest. Suddenly, I heard a distant crash similar to the sound of broken glass. Strangely enough, the apparent struggle stopped the moment I listened to the crash. As I continued to listen, waiting in great anticipation of what would happen next, I overheard the cries of a woman. It sounded like a familiar voice, which I had definitely heard before. The detective side of me came to life; I rose up, determined to go and confirm if my assumptions were correct. As I searched for the nearest piece of warm clothing, I could hear Aunty Joy heading out of her bedroom. She had also decided to go and investigate what was happening outside. It was just the two of us in the house, as Tatenda had gone to work.

"So you have been awake too?" Aunty Joy asked when she saw me making my way to the living room. "Yes, those noises were very intense tonight and it strangely sounds like Sarah who is crying outside," I said as I reached out to open the front door. We both stepped outside and it was chillingly cold. I couldn't help but grind my teeth as the ice-cold breeze brushed across my face. Just as we had predicted, the sounds were indeed coming from Sarah and Dave's house. Sarah was standing at her doorstep, sobbing uncontrollably. As we reached her, we could see the bloody bruises all over her beautiful face. At first glance, we couldn't tell if she was trembling with fear or from the cold that was raging outside.

"My dear Sarah, what's wrong?" Aunty Joy asked in a concerned tone, resisting the inclination to hold Sarah's hand now that we were in the middle of a pandemic.

"I can't... keep quiet about this... anymore," Sarah replied in between sobs. "Dave has been physically and emotionally abusing me, for many years. No one knew the tough time I've been experiencing. With all the money and being pampered from time to time, I faked happiness, yet deep down I was suffering. The pandemic has made the situation far worse as Dave now spends most of his time at home. Atleast before, he would spend the entire day at work, which left me with some room to breathe. With him in the house all day long, I feel physically and mentally trapped. Tonight the fight was so bad that I thought Dave was going to finally kill me. That's when I grabbed a nearby vase and struck him in the head. He's lying unconscious on the floor. I don't know what he'll do to me when he wakes up, considering I've never fought back every time he beat me..." Sarah's words broke off and she started crying profusely again. "Please don't leave me here alone with him, implored Sarah as she attempted to hold onto Aunty Joy's arm, who was trying to politely resist any close contact, given that the virus was running rampant. "We'll get help and nothing bad will happen to you," Aunty Joy reassured her. As for her kids, they were somehow still fast asleep and Dave hadn't attempted to harm them in any way. I breathed a sigh of relief, knowing that nothing had happened to the innocent kids.

As per Aunty Joy's instructions, I called the emergency hotline expeditiously, and within minutes, a police car and an ambulance arrived. When they finally arrived, Dave was still unconscious but alive. Sarah was called in for questioning and she explained that the attack was all in self-defense. The police still needed to investigate further, but fortunately, Sarah wasn't arrested that evening. She was understandably too traumatized to go back and sleep in that big house. We were given the permission to enter the house and collect the kids, who were strangely still asleep regardless of the commotion. Aunty Joy wanted to offer her and the kids a place to stay but sadly this wasn't possible. With the government rules which prohibited different households from mixing in place, Sarah and her children had to spend some days staying at a nearby hotel.

As I finally managed to get some rest early that morning, I shuddered at the thought of what Sarah had been enduring all these years. Although Aunty Joy and I had been quick to dismiss

Tatenda's inclinations regarding Sarah's behavior, he had been right all along. No one knew what went on behind closed doors, so it was best to not admire or pass judgment on someone you knew very little of. Sarah was sadly a victim of domestic violence. She understandably, had been afraid of people's reactions if they discovered that her life was not as "glittery" and perfect as they envisioned. Now that she had almost died in one of the worst fights with her husband, it was hard to hide the truth. Although invisible, the pain in her heart wouldn't let her continue pretending she was happy. With barely any qualifications or work experience, she knew life without the financial support of her husband; Dave was going to be difficult. But as the saying goes "there is no force more powerful than a woman determined to rise." She picked herself up from the ashes and fearlessly reached for the stars. The journey to freedom was not going to be easy or quick but day by day, brick by brick she began to create a better life for herself and her children. Her desire was to be happy, have a piece of mind and start life afresh without living in constant fear of Dave's abusive and erratic behavior.

Sadly, Sarah isn't the only victim, as the statistics show that 1 in 3 women globally experience violence. She was one of those who found help in the nick of time; who knows what would have happened to her if she didn't successfully defend herself and rushed outside? Unfortunately, throughout the global pandemic we have heard numerous news reports of increasing domestic abuse cases against women worldwide.

CHAPTER FIVE:

COVID ROBBED MY INNOCENCE

I had been in staying in London for almost six weeks and the never-ending cycle of lockdowns, social distance rules etc. were all starting to push me off the edge. To make the situation worse, we were all still trying to get our heads around Sarah's situation, how it had been happening right under our noses. All this really made me miss home, my sister especially. We always had our legendary fights, but time apart always made us realize that there was nothing better than a sisterly bond. She was my best friend, annoying but incredibly clever and hilarious too! Although we had a big age gap, she was one of my inspirations; I admired her determination and fearlessness. While young girls her own age were busy parading the streets of Harare after school in their mini-skirts trying to get male attention, Farai would always head straight home. She was studious, always getting the top grades, as her dream was to become a pilot. "No one wants to board a plane knowing that the pilot barely passed their exams when they were at school," Farai would often say jokingly.

However, when the lockdown was enforced, which led to school closures amongst other public facilities, many students resorted to doing their studies online. Most parents, especially my mum, were very concerned about how this would affect their children's future, considering that not every child functions well in a home school environment. In most parts of the world, like Zimbabwe, where it's expensive to access electricity and the internet, online education meant that children from poorer households missed lessons. While some seemed to thrive even with the drastic changes, the same cannot be said for all students. A home is supposed to be a safe space/environment, but sadly this isn't the case for many young people who are subjected to exploitation and violence by family members. Going to school is usually a perfect escape, which allows them to forget about the chaos back at home.

Farai had always been a high achiever, but she struggled with this new way of learning, which reflected in her average grades. She thrived in a classroom environment and really missed interacting with other students. Thankfully we had our neighbour Mr.Zuva, a widower and retired university professor who had generously offered to provide Farai with some extra lessons. His only daughter and Farai attended the same classes, so it made sense for him to assist them both. When the lockdown restrictions were eased, Farai would go over to Mr. Zuva's home on Tuesdays and Thursdays to have extra maths and chemistry lessons. This was a welcome relief for my mum as she became increasingly concerned about Farai's poor academic performance. Being the owner of a busy private medical clinic, she barely had time to sit down and help Farai with her school assignments. She had taken over the business following our father's death and was doing very well, much to the surprise of many.

At home, we had our lovely housemaid, Aunty Bertha, a fascinating character to say the least! She had been hired to assist with the house chores, so most of her days were spent cleaning, cooking, and ensuring that Farai had gone and returned from school on time. As lovely as she was, our housemaid was not in a position to assist Farai with the more complicated stuff like algebra or chemistry. She would often jokingly say to us, "I barely passed my grade one studies, so please don't ask me to help you unless it involves questions on child-rearing, farming, or cleaning."

Weeks went by, and the government continued to extend the lockdown, which meant that schools and other public places remained closed. Much to everyone's surprise, Farai who had been complaining about missing going into school, seemed to have had a change of heart. She seemed to be enjoying having her extra lessons at Mr. Zuva's home twice a week. However, as time went on, Farai's attitude and behaviour began to change for the worse. Aunty Bertha informed me how she no longer listened to mum's instructions and was starting to dress more provocatively especially for a young girl her age. When I would ring to check on how the family was doing, the usually jovial and talkative Farai, who always had stories to tell me, had weirdly gone mute. Every answer was just a yes or no, which got me very concerned. At first, I was convinced that she was just being a teenager, but surely, she couldn't have had a personality transplant within such a short space of time. Mr.Zuva requested that she spend more time with him, doing extra lessons. According to him this would greatly increase Farai's chances of securing an internship at his friend's school for young pilots. His interest in Farai was very unusual, but no one at home had taken any notice of this; after all, he was kindly dedicating a substantial amount of his time to make sure that she achieved excellent grades.

As I would later come to learn, Farai started returning home later than usual, despite Mr. Zuva's home being across the street from ours. Her attitude and behaviour didn't get any better. When mum questioned her about coming home late, she said that schoolwork was becoming more demanding and Mr. Zuva suggested that she finished her assignments before returning home. As much as my mum wanted to believe her, she knew that something else was causing Farai to be late. With her provocative dressing and minimal conversation she was convinced that someone was badly influencing her. She urgently wanted to confront Mr.Zuva, but changed her mind once Farai began coming back home on time. Still, she would spend most of her time locked away in her room, only coming out for a meal and interacting briefly with mum. How could her once bubbly and respectful daughter change character all of a sudden?

One evening, I received a call from Aunty Bertha explaining to me how mum had finally sat down to speak with Farai over her bad attitude. She recalled how, Farai was coming out with all types of excuses, but on that particular evening mum had refused to fall for her calculated lies. Her decision to have an open, honest conversation with Farai was final and she could not escape to her room as per usual. We later realized that if this conversation had happened earlier, Farai's life would not have been forever changed by the unacceptable experience she went through under the hands of Mr.Zuva. Amid tears, Farai revealed that Mr.Zuva had become strangely interested in her a few weeks after she began taking extra lessons from him. She recalled how he would persuade her to spend some time with him in private after the lessons. The man usually sent his daughter to do the house chores and used this opportunity to express his admiration for Farai.

Being a naive teenager, Farai believed everything Mr.Zuva told her and that's the moment her behaviour started changing. During the private time with Mr.Zuva, Farai said he would move closer to her, touching her inappropriately. She admitted she was uncomfortable with his advances. When she tried to resist, Mr. Zuva appeared disappointed and almost got angry with her. It turned out that he was the one who 'advised' her to start dressing skimpily, 'for him.' I listened in shock while mum recounted everything my sister had told her. Farai found it hard to confide in anyone about Mr Zuva's highly inappropriate behaviour towards her. Instead, she had resorted to spending most of the time alone in her room, chatting late into the night with her friends on social media. As a result, her grades didn't improve much, even with the extra lessons provided by Mr.Zuva. To mum's utter dismay; Farai revealed that Mr.Zuva went on to have sexual relations with her several days after he began touching her. Scared of what people would say if they discovered what she had been going through, Farai decided to keep it to herself, not telling a single soul.

As much as mum was furious at Mr.Zuva for sexually abusing Farai, she was relieved that my sister was bold enough to say everything he had subjected her to. It was heartbreaking to learn that a man old enough to be her father had taken away her innocence. I had heard stories of young girls being taken advantage of by older men, but to think that my sister was now a victim tore me apart. Sadly, at the height of the pandemic, cases of abuse towards young girls increased significantly and so did the number of teenage pregnancies and child marriages. Many young girls who had stopped attending classes when schools were closed down became the target of sexually abusive men. It is said that the girls would be lured into the hands of predators by gifts, clothes and money. The men would promise to care for their needs or even marry them, only to walk away when the girls got pregnant. Some girls would be forced to have unsafe abortions and sadly lose their lives in the process. Others would be married off at a young age with the consent of their parents, primarily because of poverty.

A month later, my mother phoned me crying profusely after finding out that Farai was pregnant with Mr. Zuva's child. This was disheartening to hear; her life had been disrupted, her innocence was gone and her academic performance was not encouraging either. Discovering that she was pregnant made Farai so devastated that she had trouble studying, could hardly eat or even get out of the house for some fresh air. Although victims of such cases were often fearful to report them, both Farai and mum were relentless in ensuring justice was served. They decided to take legal action against Mr.Zuva, but due to the restrictions caused by Covid-19, the case is still on-going.

CHAPTER SIX:

———∞———

AT DEATH'S DOOR

"I'm beyond drained, we lost five patients today and 10 are currently on ventilators," Tatenda expressed sorrowfully. Across most parts of the world, hospitals were overburdened with many Covid-19 patients, which evidently took its toll on the staff. There were times when Tatenda would return home after two days, looking absolutely shattered and soulless.

After two months, the virus was still at its peak across Europe. As a result, restrictions remained in place, and the government had banned international travel to most parts of the world. This ban meant that my stay in London would be extended again. While I loved the company of Aunty Joy and Tatenda, I was starting to feel homesick. I missed spending time with my loved ones but had accepted the situation and decided to adjust to the new way of living. Whenever we went out for a walk or to the nearby shops, Aunty Joy always reminded me to be careful. "Don't forget to wear your mask and keep a safe distance away from everyone," she warned me repeatedly. We observed these precautions, and being a prayerful woman, Aunt Joy prayed to God that none of us would get infected with the virus.

Since we faithfully followed all the rules, I believed we had nothing much to worry about until one day Aunty Joy started complaining of feeling very weak. "Aunty, are you okay?" I asked. "Yes dear, don't worry about me," she responded unconvincingly. "I'm just exhausted, but nothing to be concerned about; some rest will rejuvenate me." Apart from feeling exhausted, Aunty Joy didn't have any other alarming symptoms, so we assumed that she would be okay after getting some rest. However, the next day she unusually came to wake me up very early in the morning. I immediately sensed that something was wrong. She complained of joint pain, a dry cough and decided to take some paracetamol which helped her rest for a couple of hours.

That evening when Tatenda arrived back from work, he didn't want to take any chances and urgently requested Aunty to isolate away from us and take a Covid-19 test. Sadly, the results returned positive, which sent chills of apprehension down our spines.

She was immediately restricted to her bedroom and had to refrain from coming into contact with anyone else for a while. My heart started racing in fear, considering that the virus was highly transmissible. For the past few weeks, Tatenda and I had freely interacted with her, utterly oblivious to the fact that she was carrying the virus. "Fear not, I'm going to be okay; let's keep the faith," she reassured us.

Although we were living in the same house, we maintained our distance. I moved to the guest room downstairs while Aunty Joy stayed in her bedroom, which thankfully had its own bathroom. We communicated via the phone, so I would call to check on her every few hours. All seemed to be okay until one afternoon, when she managed to call me complaining about having breathing difficulties. "I'm having trouble breathing; it feels as if something heavy is sitting on my chest," she said, gasping for air in between words. My heart sank for a minute and many thoughts rushed through my mind. We'd seen images of patients lying in the hospital wards, breathing with the help of ventilators. The idea of Aunty Joy, being one of them, filled me with great anxiety. Across the UK, hospitals were advising people with Covid-19 symptoms to isolate at home, but this was a severe situation requiring a medical professional's attention. Fortunately, Tatenda arrived back from work just in time and called the ambulance immediately.

A few moments later, we stood outside as we watched her being carried off in an ambulance. She was a strong woman who knew how to fight with everything she had. Now more than ever, her faith would be instrumental in contributing to her healing. Although the unexpected happened, our faith in God gave us hope to fight and maintain a positive attitude. I called the family back in Harare and informed them about Aunty Joy's condition. They promised to pray for her and encouraged us to have unwavering faith. When we received a phone call from the doctors attending to her, we soon realized that we needed to be stronger than ever.

Her situation had deteriorated, which meant we couldn't see or communicate with her for a while. No visitors were allowed in the ward to minimize the risk of transmission. My world began to crumble right before my eyes as I also discovered that Tatenda's struggle with depression and anxiety had escalated. He encountered occasional episodes of anxiety attacks and the symptoms mimicked those of a heart attack. Eating and other seemingly simple tasks became a struggle for him. Little did I know that the worst was still yet to come.

Two days later, a wave of fear engulfed us when we received a discouraging report from the doctors. Aunty Joy was still in a bad condition and her lungs were on the verge of collapsing. This information was heart-rending, but I had to hold onto the little strength and faith I had left. If one of us could gather strength and fight, there was a possibility that we would conquer it all. I encouraged Tatenda to continue believing that God would heal Aunty Joy, no matter the severity of her situation. We prayed earnestly for divine intervention; asking God to graciously preserve her life. Unfortunately, many people that had been seriously affected by the virus never made it out of the hospital alive. BUT, as the bible teaches us that God can do exceedingly and abundantly, we indeed made this word the center of our meditation. A few days later, we experienced God's power like never before, which lifted our spirits and kept our hope alive. The doctors attending to Aunty Joy told us how her situation had drastically improved. She was now able to breathe for longer periods without the assistance of a ventilator. "God, you're amazing," I rejoiced as I grabbed my phone to call my family in Harare and share the great news.

Even amidst his own internal battles, Tatenda had made great efforts to be strong for his mum. We had decided to join a virtual prayer group set up by some of Aunty Joy's friends. Online prayer sessions were held every evening, which helped us remain hopeful and continue trusting God regardless of the upsetting situation. We felt more hopeful when two people testified how God had healed their relatives from severe Covid-19. This strengthened our faith, and we began to believe that a miraculous breakthrough was imminent. The fellowship we had in the virtual prayer group was powerful. To be frank, it wasn't easy being in a foreign country with an Aunty at death's door and knowing that back home in Harare, my teenage sister had been impregnated by a man almost thrice her age. This was definitely not what I had signed up for when I boarded the flight to London. I had envisioned us having a wonderful time, bonding, and just enjoying life. Our good time had suddenly been interrupted by Covid-19.

At this point, God was indeed our only hope, as a viable vaccine hadn't been developed yet. I didn't even want to begin to imagine what this mysterious virus was capable of doing to someone's body. The media had started publishing articles on Covid-19; some titled 'What Covid-19 Does to Your Body.' The title was scary enough, and I decided not to focus on what the media was saying but on what God could do. Tatenda and I continued attending the virtual prayer group, and our miracle finally happened. I firmly believed that it was the power of prayer, faith, fellowship, and positivity which caused Aunty Joy's situation to improve miraculously. Within a week, she was transferred from the intensive care unit to the main ward. We were; however shocked to learn that she was the only person to have been released from the ward alive and well. All the other patients had sadly succumbed to the virus. The day we went to pick her up from the hospital was a day full of joy; she could walk, talk, and breathe all by herself. A follow-up appointment at the hospital confirmed that her lungs were once again healthy and functional. Although we couldn't go to church physically and testify, we gave our testimony during the next meeting at our virtual prayer group. Those going through trying times felt encouraged, as her life was indeed a testament to God's unfailing grace.

"I appreciate how you and my son prayed for me constantly without ceasing," she said with a sigh of relief after a moment's reflection. "I will never laugh again when you tell us to use anointing oil to chase away evil spirits," Tatenda chimed in. We were filled with joy and gratitude; all was okay at last. To my surprise, I had somehow managed to remain free from the virus which was a huge relief. A couple weeks later, the government allowed people to travel only if they would stay in quarantine for 14 days upon reaching their destination. Upon hearing this news, I boarded a plane back to Harare. This had not been an ordinary trip; it took many unexpected turns but I surely went home stronger, wiser, and more prayerful. If there was one great lesson I learnt, it was to value and prioritize my relationship with God. To have active communication with him, open up my heart and rely entirely on him. As one preacher perfectly said, "look to God as your main source; he's the only one that can take you out of the darkness and deliver you into light, transform your pain into power, lack to abundance."

It is in our struggles and our darkest moments that we grow the most in Christ. Don't despise hardships but allow God to use them as a training ground to build up your faith and draw you closer to him.

Printed in Great Britain
by Amazon